Sandy Lane Stables

Sandy Lane Stables

Dream Pony

Susannah Leigh

Adapted by: Katie Daynes

Reading consultant: Alison Kelly

Series editor: Lesley Sims

Designed by: Brenda Cole

Cover and inside illustrations: Barbara Bongini

Map illustrations: John Woodcock

This edition first published in 2016 by Usborne Publishing Ltd.,
Usborne House, 83-85 Saffron Hill, London EC1N 8RT, England.
www.usborne.com

Contents

1.   No Riding Today   7

2.   Ponies and Rychester   13

3.   The Unfairness of Life   23

4.   No More Sandy Lane?   30

5.   Rychester   37

6.   Dream Pony   44

7.   Jump Disaster   52

8.   Things Get Better   59

9.   Jess Moves On   72

10.   Friends Old and New   77

11.   The Competition Looms   89

12.   Jess Has Doubts   97

13.   Revelations   103

14.   Dilemma   107

15.   Nightmare   113

16.   Showdown   120

17.   Home at Last   126

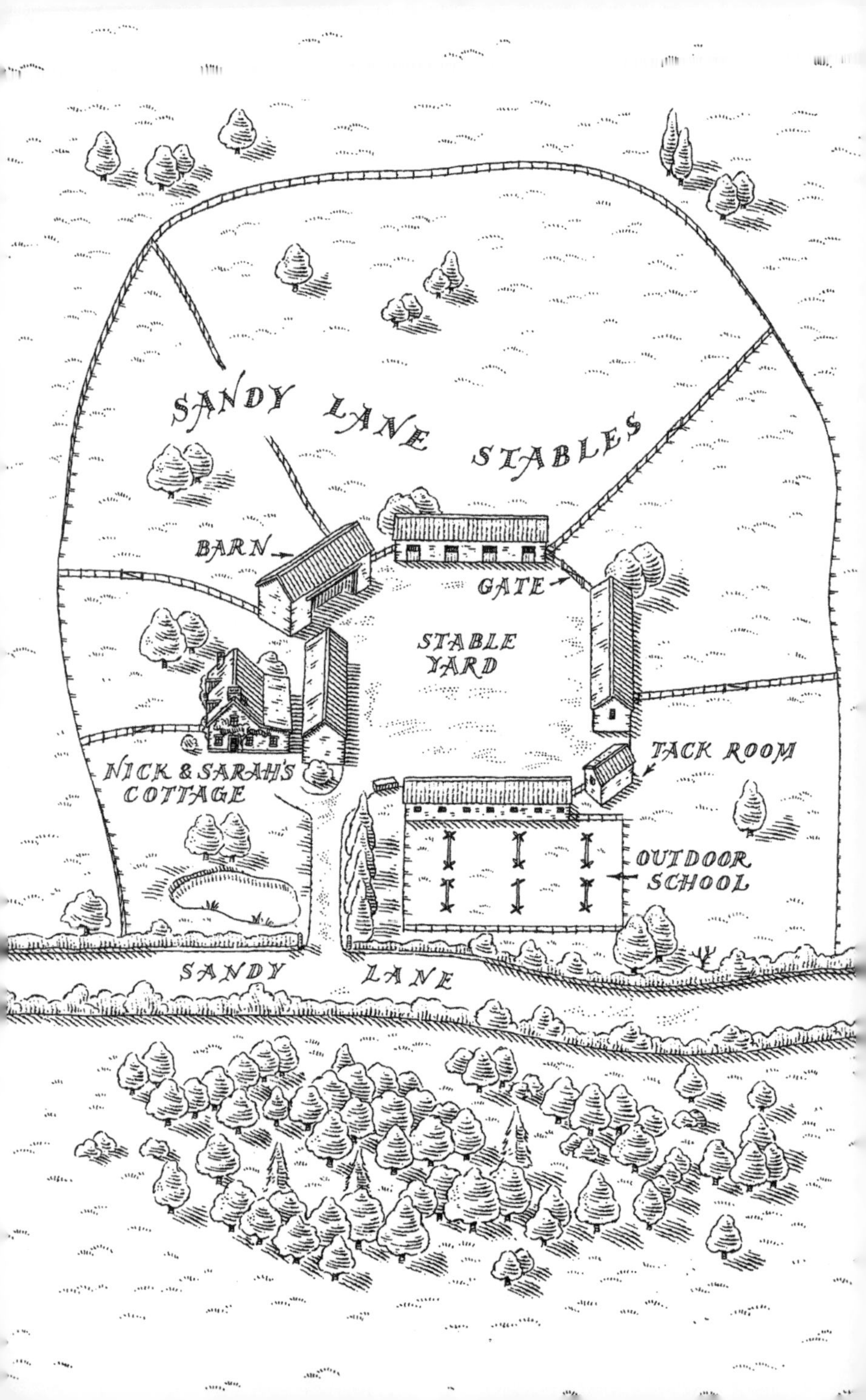

SANDY LANE STABLES

BARN

GATE

STABLE YARD

NICK & SARAH'S COTTAGE

TACK ROOM

OUTDOOR SCHOOL

SANDY LANE

Chapter 1

No Riding Today

"Well, we could play a game of cards," Rosie Edwards suggested, looking up from the pony magazine she had been idly skimming through.

"Boring," her friend Jess Adams answered. "Oh when will it ever stop raining?" She hunched closer to Rosie and peered through the tack room window. Outside, the rain teemed down relentlessly.

"Maybe it'll clear up this afternoon," said Rosie.

Jess gazed doubtfully at the darkening sky.

The two friends had mucked out endless boxes, filled mountains of haynets and groomed the Sandy

Lane ponies till they could almost see their faces in their coats.

On any other Saturday, they would have been outside in the yard, tacking up the ponies for the 11 o'clock hack, but because of the torrential rain, Nick and Sarah Brooks, the owners of Sandy Lane, had called it off. Last Saturday's mid-morning hack had been rained off too, and Nick had cancelled the mid-week lessons because of flu, so it really wasn't a good time for Sandy Lane Stables right now.

"Rain, rain, go away," Jess sang grumpily. She pulled a sheet of paper out of her bag. "I was going to fill this in later, but I may as well do it now."

"What is it?" Rosie looked up.

"An entry form for the *Win a Dream Pony Competition*. I picked it up from the shopping centre when I was buying school shoes with my mum." Jess smiled and showed it to Rosie. "What are my chances of winning?" She laughed.

"Pretty slim," Rosie admitted, grinning. "Anyway, you don't need to win a pony – not when you've got all the Sandy Lane ones. I can't imagine wanting to ride any other pony but Pepper."

Jess sighed. "You're very loyal, Rosie," she said. Pepper was one of Sandy Lane's oldest ponies, a stubborn little piebald that Rosie adored. "Of course the Sandy Lane horses are great, but it's not the same as having one of your very own."

"Well, it's good enough for me," Rosie answered firmly. "Still, we've nothing better to do. What do you have to do to win?"

Jess grabbed a pen and read the first question. "Name six points of the horse. Hmm – tendons, pastern, fetlocks…" She stopped and chewed her pen thoughtfully.

"Withers, croup, hocks," Rosie finished quickly.

"Pretty good," Jess said. "Hey, listen to this. The runners-up will win a year's supply of New Improved Mango Miracle Shampoo, and a bottle of Essence of Peach Perfume, courtesy of competition sponsors Vrai Vert Cosmetics. Yuck." Jess wrinkled up her nose. "Who'd want to win that?"

"Natural ingredients…" Rosie glanced down the page, reading bits aloud. "A caring company… No animal testing… That's good to hear."

"It certainly is," Jess declared. "But Essence of Ponies is the only smell for me."

Rosie laughed and Jess grinned back at her friend. They couldn't look more different if they tried. Rosie was always beautifully turned out: the buttons on her jacket were never missing; there were never holes in her socks; her hair was never messy or uncombed.

Not like me, Jess thought. Strange then, that she and Rosie should be best friends. But there was one thing they shared with a passion – a love of horses and ponies in all shapes and sizes.

Jess sighed heavily as she looked around the cosy tack room with its moth-eaten armchairs, faded but cheerful curtains and tattered old pony magazines. This was where all the regular Sandy Lane riders congregated: Rosie and Jess of course, and their friends Charlie and Tom, Alex and his sister Kate and, more recently, Izzy Paterson. Only Jess and Rosie were mad enough to hang around Sandy Lane on a day like today. Indeed, Rosie was only here because Jess had begged her to come.

"It might clear up. You never know," Jess had observed, optimistically.

The 11 o'clock hack had been the only thing that had propelled her through a dreary week of school. Still, it wouldn't have been safe to ride in the howling storm, especially with all the wet mud under foot.

Jess and Rosie worked their way through the competition questions. They were doing quite well.

"Oh no, I knew there had to be a catch," Jess groaned. "The dreaded tiebreaker. Why do they always put them at the bottom?"

Rosie leaned over Jess's shoulder and read out the opening words. "My dream pony would be… Come on, Jess," she said. "You can finish that in less than twenty words."

"My dream pony would be…" Jess repeated the words and paused.

She knew her family would never be able to afford a pony. The only way Jess was able to ride at all was by helping out at Sandy Lane in return for free lessons. Not that she minded – she felt very lucky.

"My dream pony would be one I could ride when I was awake, not just in my dreams." Jess spoke the words as she scribbled them down.

"Not bad." Rosie smiled. "You should send it off."

"I might just do that," Jess said. "And look… it's finally stopped raining!"

Jess stuffed the competition form in her pocket and followed Rosie happily out of the tack room, into the brightening stable yard.

Chapter 2

Ponies and Rychester

Nick Brooks coughed loudly and rubbed his hands together. "Listen up, everybody," he croaked. "My throat's sore so I'll keep this short."

It was the following Saturday and the 11 o'clock hack was ready to go. Rosie was on her beloved Pepper. Alex Hardy was on Hector, a huge horse of 16 hands, and his sister Kate rode the grey Arab, Feather. Charlie Marshall was on Napoleon and Tom Buchanan was riding his own horse, Chancey, a beautiful chestnut gelding. Izzy was on Midnight and Jess was riding Minstrel, Sandy Lane's reliable skewbald pony. The ponies shifted restlessly as an icy wind blew through the yard.

"It's been a tough winter, what with the new stables being set up down the road and lessons here having to be cancelled," Nick continued.

The riders all shifted uncomfortably in their saddles. Rychester Riding Stables had been running for about a month now and already a number of Sandy Lane riders had disappeared from the books. Jess didn't like to see Nick looking so worried.

"Anyway, I won't be able to take you out for a hack now. I need to crack on with lessons here," Nick said briskly. "We don't want to lose any more riders to Rychester. However, as a thank you for all the hard work you've put in recently, I'm happy for you to go out on your own if you want to."

"Oh, yes please!" the riders cried in unison.

"Right, well Tom's in charge. The ground's pretty frozen, so take it easy. I don't want any of you breaking your necks." Nick turned on his heels and headed off.

One by one, the riders followed Tom out of the yard. As soon as they turned into Sandy Lane the little group was hit by gusts of wind. The ponies' ears twitched and their tails flicked up and down. Chancey began side-stepping and prancing around.

"We'll take the coastal track up past Bucknell Woods," Tom bellowed back to the others. "These ponies have got the wind up, so hold on tight."

Tom urged Chancey into a brisk trot and the others copied. The rhythmic rising in the saddle, the clopping of hooves and the ponies' snorts brought comfort against the fierce wind. Jess bent down and patted Minstrel's thick, shaggy neck.

"It's good to be out again, isn't it, old boy? Don't worry, we'll take it slowly. It's not a day for galloping."

Minstrel pricked up his ears and tossed his intelligent head as if he understood. Jess remembered the times when, feeling low, she had crept into his stable, snuggled her face into his mane and told him her troubles. He had always made her feel better.

The riders picked their way along the cliff path

above Sandy Bay. Giant waves thundered against the shore and sand swirled in the air as the grassy dunes were whipped by the ferocious gusts. Jess pulled in the reins and kept them short. The sound and sight of the sea had lathered the ponies into a frenzy of excitement, and the riders needed all their strength and skill to hold them back.

Once past Larkfield Copse, Tom suggested they stay in single file, well away from the cliff edge. The horses stumbled occasionally on the bumpy frozen path, but they had calmed down a little now. Jess was watching a small boat near the lighthouse, appearing and disappearing in the raging sea, when suddenly she felt Minstrel stiffen beneath her. He must have sensed something. She looked back and noticed several dots haring towards them.

"Something's coming our way!" Jess shouted.

The other riders strained their necks to see and Tom held up his hand to halt the ride.

It was now obvious that they were looking at a group of horses and riders, galloping at top speed.

Jess could see that the horses were pure-bred beauties. They charged up to the Sandy Lane riders, and swerved past them, right at the cliff's edge.

"Stupid, dangerous idiots!" Tom shouted after the riders, holding tight onto Chancey's reins. Jess and the others were trying to calm their own ponies who were now cavorting, electrified, and trying to join in the race.

"They are CRAZY!" Jess shouted to the others, but secretly she couldn't help feeling a rush of admiration for the daring riders.

"Don't let the horses look," Tom yelled. "Come on, let's go."

And quickly the Sandy Lane riders set off once more, struggling to keep their ponies at a walk. The wind had changed direction now and was blowing hard in their faces. Jess was really starting to feel the cold. Her hands were so numb she could hardly keep a grip on the reins. Carefully they picked their way past the lighthouse towards Sandy Lane Cove.

"What was all that about?" Jess asked, trotting

alongside Rosie. "Who were those mad riders? Do you think they're from the new stables?"

"What, Rychester? They looked completely out of control to me," Rosie snorted.

"I suppose so," Jess agreed slowly. "But those horses were amazing, weren't they? Did you notice the palomino out in front? He was superb."

"Hmm, fancy getting to ride a horse like that and being so stupid with it," Rosie replied grimly. "Gosh, was that thunder?"

Jess had heard a rumble too, but it wasn't thunder. It was the sound of pounding hooves, carried by the wind. The pure-bred horses were heading back their way. This time, the wild group slowed to a trot before passing the Sandy Lane riders. A blonde-haired girl on the palomino shot Jess and Rosie a look which clearly indicated she considered them to be inferior. Then she dug her heels into her horse's side and galloped away, her fellow riders following at a pace.

The Sandy Lane riders sat and watched quietly.

Tom was the first to break the silence. "Come on,

you lot, let's go," he said.

The others walked on behind him. Jess couldn't resist stopping for just a second to look back at the tiny dots disappearing into the darkening sky.

The following Saturday, Jess and Rosie sat in the tack room at Sandy Lane, cleaning saddles and discussing the Ash Hill Show, the next big event on the local horsey calendar.

"Of course you'll be riding at Ash Hill, Jess," Rosie was reassuring her, but Jess wasn't convinced.

"There's no one left for me to ride!" she pointed out. "Charlie will be riding Napoleon and of course Tom will be on Chancey. I suppose Kate will enter a show class with Feather and Alex will probably go for the Working Hunter on Hector. Maybe Nick would let me enter Minstrel, but he hasn't really got a chance of winning anything... Oh, if only Storm Cloud wasn't lame."

"Poor old Jess," said Rosie sympathetically.

"What class are you down for?" asked Jess.

"I'm riding Pepper in the Open Jumping," Rosie replied. "I bet those awful girls from the cliffs have enough ponies to ride," she added.

Last Saturday's encounter with the riders on the clifftop had been the talk of the stable yard. A quick check with some ex-Sandy Lane riders had confirmed that they were from Rychester. Everyone agreed they were a reckless bunch, but there was no denying their horses looked wonderful.

"Nick's rather worried about Rychester, isn't he?" Jess observed, thinking of the beautiful palomino pony they'd seen.

"I guess so," Rosie said. "Although why anyone would want to ride anywhere other than Sandy Lane, I don't know," she added, defensively.

"Susie Matthews and Emma James went on a Rychester hack last week and said it was brilliant," Jess remarked. "They came back full of it – how clean and smart Rychester was, how beautiful and responsive the ponies were, how they'd gone on a really fast ride..."

"How they almost broke their necks, how expensive their hack was, how everyone was really snooty," Rosie finished, grinning.

"Maybe." Jess laughed along with her friend. "But you must admit, they were all pretty good riders. A bit dangerous perhaps, but certainly daring."

"Well, you've always been more adventurous than me, Jess." Rosie sighed. "But do you really think Rychester is a threat to Sandy Lane?"

"It definitely sounds that way," Jess replied grimly. "Money's always tight here and, with Storm Cloud being lame, Nick hasn't got as many horses to hire out as before. Then there are the lessons cancelled because of the bad weather... Apparently Rychester has an indoor school, and it's full-sized!"

"Luxury!" Rosie said.

Jess looked around the scruffy tack room, and down at the worn bridle she was cleaning. "You know, if I didn't love Sandy Lane so much, I'd probably think it was rather run-down."

"It's not run-down, it's just..." Rosie searched for

the right words. "Lived-in, that's all!"

"What's lived-in?" A voice behind them made them jump. They whipped around to see Nick standing at the doorway.

"Oh nothing, Nick." Rosie blushed furiously. She wondered how much he had heard. But Nick was smiling at them.

"Well done, you two." He entered the tack room and indicated the pile of polished tack on the table. "I think there's enough there to add up to a lesson at 2 o'clock for you both. If you want one that is."

"Oh yes please!" Jess and Rosie cried at once.

"Good. I'll see you later in the outdoor school then." And he was gone.

"Do you think he heard?" Jess whispered.

"I don't think so," Rosie reassured her. "Anyway, Sandy Lane isn't about to fall apart just yet. But that bridle will if you don't get some saddle soap on it!"

Chapter 3

The Unfairness of Life

"So you didn't win the competition then," Jack announced looking down at his tablet.

"What's that?" Jess asked, peering over her brother's shoulder.

"You didn't win your precious dream pony." Jack grinned annoyingly.

"Let me see." Jess scowled. She read aloud from the screen. "Local girl, Amanda Fisher, twelve years old and now the proud owner of her dream pony…" Jess let out a long sigh.

"Ah, the unfairness of life." Jack jumped up and

grabbed his coat from the back of his chair. "The Jess Adamses of this world never win the competitions. It's always the Amanda Fishers." He was out of the door before Jess had time to throw a cushion at him.

At school the next day, Rosie mentioned the competition too. "The pony's been won by someone local. Lucky girl, whoever she is."

"Isn't she just?" Jess replied. "Of course I knew I wouldn't win, but there was no harm in hoping."

Rosie smiled sympathetically as Jess shrugged her shoulders and moved on in the lunch queue.

"At least we've got a two hour hack on Saturday to look forward to," Rosie said, sliding her tray along the canteen shelf and putting a plate of salad on it.

"That's true." Jess grinned, piling her plate with chips. "Things aren't so bad, are they?"

"Jess Adams!" Miss Gregory, the maths teacher, appeared at her elbow. "If I don't see your homework on my desk by the end of the lunchbreak you'll be doing it after school under my supervision."

Jess made a face at the teacher's departing back and Rosie giggled. "Come on, it's not too hard," she whispered. "I'll help you finish it."

With Rosie's help, Jess just managed to hand her maths homework in on time, and then they had double English till the end of the day.

"Very good, Jess," the English teacher, Mrs. Peters, commented, pointing at the pony doodles on Jess's pad. "I'm sure you'll make an excellent artist."

"What? Oh–" Jess reddened. "I-I–"

"Just don't let me catch you doing it again." But Mrs. Peters was smiling as she walked up to the front of the classroom. Ddrrrriinnnnngg! It was the bell for the end of school.

"Sorry, Miss," Jess mumbled. She packed up her things and hurried out to catch the bus home.

As Jess turned down the path to the ramshackle old cottage where she lived, her mother opened the front door.

"Quick, Jess," she called, waving the phone in her hand. "It's for you."

Jess took the phone suspiciously. "Hello?"

"Is that Jess Adams?" said a friendly female voice at the other end. "I'm phoning from Blackford's Department Store. You recently entered our 'Win a Dream Pony Competition' – the one sponsored by Vrai Vert Cosmetics?"

"Yes I did," Jess said, her heart beating faster.

"Well, congratulations," the voice continued. "You're now the proud owner of that pony."

"What?" Jess's heart was in her mouth. "But I-I thought someone called Amanda Fisher won it. It said so on the website."

"It did," the woman said. "Only unfortunately we've just found out that her parents hadn't given their permission."

Jess's heart started to beat faster. "But didn't they sign the entry form?" she asked.

"I'm afraid that Amanda Fisher forged her mother's signature," the woman explained. "And her parents don't want her to have a pony. So that disqualifies her. It's very sad for her, but good news for you as first runner-up."

Good news for you. The words rang in Jess's ear.

"Jess, are you there?" the woman asked.

"Yes, yes, I'm here," Jess said excitedly.

"Well, I was going to be phoning you anyway about winning the runners-up beauty products," the woman explained. "But I'm afraid this means you won't be getting them now."

Jess almost laughed out loud. Imagine Rosie's face if she had won those!

"Your mother's confirmed that her signature on your form was genuine," continued the woman. "Of course there's free stabling for a year at Rychester Riding Stables and the pony's tack is part of the prize too. Anyway, I've popped all the details in the post. You should get them tomorrow. So, well done Jess. Jess? Hello? Are you still there?"

Jess was still stumbling over one word the woman had said – *Rychester*. Had she heard correctly? Jess stood rooted to the spot, butterflies darting and spiralling in her stomach.

"But I ride at Sandy Lane Stables," she stated slowly. "Can't I keep the pony there?"

"I'm sorry, that's not possible," the woman said. "The deal's already been arranged."

"But couldn't it be changed?" Jess pushed, starting to panic.

"No, I'm afraid not."

"Oh." Jess didn't know what to say. It was a dream come true to have won a pony, but to have to stable it somewhere other than Sandy Lane, and worse still – Rychester...

Jess quickly pulled herself to her senses. She was being silly. Here she was, being handed a prize pony on a plate, and she was arguing about the stabling. How selfish of her!

"Rychester it is then. Thank you," Jess said, remembering her manners.

Gently her mother took the phone. From what seemed like miles away Jess could hear her mother's voice, wrapping up the conversation.

"Yes, thanks for ringing. We'll wait for the details.

Of course Jess will be happy to do some publicity photo-shots. Yes that would be great. Speak to you soon. Goodbye."

"Well!" she said, turning to Jess. "I'd never have signed that form if I thought there was a chance you'd actually win the wretched thing. I don't know what we'll do when the year's up and the free stabling comes to an end, but I suppose we'll just have to cross that bridge when we come to it."

Jess's mother was smiling as she spoke, and Jess could see she wasn't cross. "Just imagine your father's face when we tell him you've won a pony."

Jess let out a whoop of delight and flung her arms around her mother. "A pony!" she cried. "My very own pony! I can't believe it. This is the happiest day of my life. It's a dream come true."

Chapter 4

No More Sandy Lane?

Jess read the letter through again. She had already read it twice, but it was only now as she read it a third time, that it all really sank in.

"Congratulations Jess," it said. "You are the lucky winner of the Blackford's & Vrai Vert Cosmetics dream pony. Your pony will be arriving on Saturday March 1st at 11 o'clock at Rychester Riding Stables, Rychester, near Colcott, where it will be stabled for a year, free of charge. We have arranged a time for you to look around your pony's new home the Sunday before its arrival."

Then in smaller type was something about giving permission for photographs and a lot of legal looking instructions. Jess didn't look very closely at that. She was too excited. If only she could keep the pony at Sandy Lane then everything would be perfect.

She remembered Nick's worried face when he'd been telling them about Rychester. Whatever was he going to say when he heard about this? Maybe there was something Nick could do. Just maybe he'd be able to persuade the competition organizers to let her stable her pony at Sandy Lane.

Jess checked her phone. It was already half past one and she'd promised to meet Rosie at Sandy Lane at two. She'd only managed to send Rosie a quick text so far and her friend would be dying to know more about the pony.

"I can't believe it!" Rosie cried as Jess cycled into the yard. "You lucky thing."

Jess dumped her bike and followed her friend's excited chatter into the tack room.

"You must tell me everything," Rosie insisted.

"I don't even know what the pony looks like yet," Jess admitted. "But I keep on imagining it. Perhaps it'll be a beautiful chestnut like Chancey. Or a black thoroughbred like Midnight."

"It might be a palomino," Rosie cried.

"I won't care if it's a shaggy little skewbald like Minstrel." Jess smiled happily.

One by one, the rest of the afternoon ride piled into the room and Jess was quick to share her news.

"Your own pony?" Kate exclaimed. "Lucky you."

"I was going to enter that competition," Alex said. "I just never got around to it."

"Congratulations." Tom grinned.

And as everyone checked their names in the ride book and gathered up tack, the questions poured in.

"So what's this pony like then, Jess?"

"When's it arriving?"

"Will you be jumping it at Ash Hill?"

"Another pony at Sandy Lane!" Rosie cheered.

Jess squirmed in her seat. "Well actually, there's a bit of a problem," she said, feeling uncomfortable.

"You see, I might not be able to stable it at Sandy Lane. It's already been arranged for the pony to be stabled somewhere else."

"Somewhere else?" The others looked on in disbelief, as if there could be no other stable in the world except Sandy Lane. "Where?"

"Um, it's Rychester actually," Jess blurted out.

"Rychester!" Rosie echoed. "Oh no, Jess."

"I know." Jess hung her head. "They said everything had been arranged already."

Jess's friends didn't know what to say.

"Well, they might have seemed like a reckless bunch, but perhaps it won't be so bad," Tom offered tentatively.

"And maybe those riders won't be so snooty in real life," Kate added.

But it was Rosie who said what the others were really thinking. "Oh Jess, you can't go to Rychester," she wailed. "What about Nick?"

"Do you think I want to go there, Rosie?" Jess interrupted her. "There's no way I want to leave

Sandy Lane. In fact, I was going to talk to Nick straight away…see if he can do anything about it." Looking determined, she leapt up from her chair.

Jess ran across to the little cottage just behind the stables where Nick and his wife Sarah lived. The door was on the latch as usual. All the Sandy Lane riders had to do was give a quick knock and push it open. Nick and Sarah were always available and always welcoming. Jess paused in the hallway to give Ebony, the black Labrador, a pat. "Nick?" she called out.

"In the kitchen," he replied.

Nick sat at the kitchen table surrounded by paperwork. "I'm doing the accounts," he said as Jess walked in.

"Oh," Jess replied, shifting from foot to foot. "Nick," she said slowly. "I've won a pony."

"A pony?" Nick sounded pleased and surprised. "Well you don't look very happy about it, Jess. That's brilliant news. Congratulations! How did you manage that?"

Quickly, Jess explained everything. "I know it's amazing, but there's a slight catch," she said, drawing her breath in sharply.

"A catch?" Nick looked at her.

"The competition organizers have arranged free stabling for a year," Jess hurried on, "only it's at Rychester Riding Stables."

"Rychester?" Nick's voice was polite and steady.

"Yes, look, it's all in this letter," Jess said handing it over. Nick started to read as Jess kept talking.

"I was hoping you might be able to phone the organizers for me…see if we could change the stables to here. It would sound better coming from you," she said.

"I don't know." Nick was doubtful. "The terms and conditions are quite clear," he said, pointing to a section of the letter.

"I know." Jess looked glum.

"Look, I'll ring them on Monday. They'll be closed over the weekend. Maybe Sarah and I could come up with something here if we could use the pony in lessons in return for stabling. Leave it with me."

"Oh thanks, Nick," Jess said, relieved.

"I'm not making any promises, Jess," Nick said seriously. "So don't go pinning your hopes on anything."

"I won't," Jess said, skipping out of the door with new resolve.

Pausing in the corner of the yard, Jess looked around her and sighed. The water in the small pond was a cloudy brown, the surface in the outdoor school was worn and patchy, one of the barn doors was hanging off its hinges, the stables were rather shabby…but Jess simply couldn't imagine being anywhere else.

Chapter 5

Rychester

Rychester Riding Stables lay a good twenty minute bike ride from Jess's house, right on the other side of Colcott. Tomorrow, Nick would be phoning the competition organizers, but there was no harm in following their instructions and looking around Rychester today. Jess had to admit that she was curious. What was so special about these stables that they could pose such a threat to Sandy Lane?

Breathless and red-faced, Jess pedalled up the drive. A rather grand, gabled house stood back from the road and beside it a wide, gravel drive swept through the gates and into the stable yard. Nervously Jess stopped her bike and looked around. She had arrived just as a hack was about to leave. Swinging confidently into the saddles of their beautifully turned out mounts, girls clad in immaculate riding clothes called cheerfully to one another.

"Dido's really lively today. I'll keep her well back," cried a girl on a delicate roan.

"Apollo's raring to go. I vote for lots of galloping!" Jess recognised the blonde-haired girl from the cliffs, calling out from the saddle of her palomino.

"You always vote for lots of galloping, Camilla!" someone else cried. "Just keep him away from Opal."

As the ride swept smartly past her, Jess was horribly aware of her own dishevelled appearance.

She gazed anxiously into the stable yard. It was lined by twelve loose boxes, gleaming white in the bright sunlight. An Arab pony hung its head from one of the doors. Two racing green horseboxes were parked to the left of the yard. Behind them, Jess could just make out the red tiled roof of a large indoor school.

"Can I help you?" A friendly-looking girl, a few years older than Jess, strode up. "Beautiful, isn't it?" The girl gave Jess a warm smile. "I'm Amy Watkins, the head stable girl. Did you want to know about riding lessons?"

"Not exactly." Jess paused. "My name's Jess Adams. I've won a pony and I was asked to come and look around the stables, only I don't know if–"

"So you're the lucky girl who's won." Amy beamed. "You must be so excited. Feel free to look around. Your pony's arriving next week, isn't she? She's going to be stabled in the loose box in the far corner."

Jess was stuck for words. Suddenly it all seemed so real. Amy knew about her pony and there was a stable already picked out for her!

"Did you say 'she'?" she quizzed Amy eagerly. "Can you tell me more about my pony?"

Amy shook her head. "I'm sorry, they don't tell me much around here. Come into the office though. There might be some details about your pony there."

She led Jess into a tidy, carpeted room. The walls were lined with red filing cabinets and hung with charts and timetables. Several high-backed chairs were grouped around a big desk. It was a far cry from Sandy Lane's little tack room which doubled as an office. Amy rummaged in drawers and glanced through the papers on the walls. After a few minutes she shook her head. "Nothing here," she said.

Jess gave a little shrug.

"Sorry," said Amy, screwing up her nose in sympathy. "You must be dying to meet your pony. I'm afraid Jasper Carlisle, Rychester's owner, isn't around at the moment. He'd know more about it."

Just then the phone on the desk rang. Amy answered brightly and then her voice changed. "Hello, Barry. Can you hang on a minute?" she said. She gave Jess a glance. "I have to take this call," she said quickly. "Why don't you go and check out that loose box while you're here?" Amy gave a hurried wave and Jess slipped out of the office.

The boxes looked smart and bright and Amy

seemed really nice and friendly. Perhaps Rychester wouldn't be such a bad thing after all. Jess felt her stomach turn somersaults of excitement as she made her way to the loose box Amy had indicated.

She pulled back the well-oiled bolt on the loose box door and stepped inside. It was large and airy with whitewashed walls and fresh straw scattered over the flagstone floor. A large, clean water trough was well-placed in one corner and opposite the door hung a net of good quality hay. As the sweet scent of hay rose up to meet her, a horse whinnied in the distance. Jess gazed back across the dazzling stable yard and suddenly Sandy Lane was forgotten. She would keep her pony here. She liked it and she was sure her pony would like it too.

Telling Nick that afternoon was the hard part.

"They've got a box for my pony and they're expecting us and everything. Of course it's not as nice as Sandy Lane and it wasn't my choice," Jess gabbled on, staring resolutely down at Nick's black riding boots. "So I guess it would probably be better to stick with Rychester…as it's all organized," she finished lamely. She looked up cautiously and caught Nick's eye for the first time.

"It's all right, Jess, you don't need to explain." Nick smiled kindly. "It's a good job you came back to tell me straight away – I'd have looked a bit silly if I'd called the competition organizers and arranged something else. Of course we'll miss seeing you at Sandy Lane."

"Oh, but I'll be back all the time," Jess cried quickly. "I'll be bringing my pony to ride here, that's for sure."

"Glad to hear it." Nick smiled. "I hope Minstrel doesn't get too jealous." He gave the little skewbald's mane a ruffle and turned to walk back to the cottage.

When he was out of sight, Jess heaved a sigh and rested her head on Minstrel's neck. The pony shifted his weight and carried on slurping noisily from the water trough.

The afternoon was unseasonably warm, but Jess still shivered inside her jacket. She had been so sure

Rychester was the perfect place for her pony, and yet now she felt a pang of guilt. Still, it wasn't as if she were leaving Sandy Lane for good, and she wouldn't have to hang out with the Rychester riders… All this she argued to herself – and to Rosie the next day at school.

"But the way those girls rode on the clifftops that day," Rosie groaned. "How could you bear to be with them, Jess?"

"I'm sure they're not all like that, Rosie," Jess insisted, trying to convince herself as much as reassure her friend. "Amy, the stable girl, is really nice and friendly."

"Well if you think Rychester is OK, then I'm sure it must be." Rosie sighed. "The main thing is for your pony to be happy."

Jess smiled at her friend. "I'm not leaving Sandy Lane for good. I'll still ride with you and Pepper."

"You'll soon forget me once you're part of the smart Rychester set," said Rosie grinning.

"No chance of that!" Jess assured her.

Chapter 6

Dream Pony

Jess could hardly believe it. Her pony was being delivered today!

"The *Daily Advertiser* will send a photographer," the lady from Blackford's Department Store had said on the phone. "You need to be at Rychester Stables for eleven."

And now it was 10 o'clock, and Jess hopped impatiently from one foot to the other as she waited for her mum to finish marking an essay.

"Come on, Mum!" she cried.

"Calm down." Her mother laughed. "All right, I'm

coming," she said, finally closing her laptop.

"It'll probably be an old nag," Jess told herself on the car journey to Rychester Stables. "It won't be beautiful. Don't expect too much."

As they pulled into the driveway, Jess's heart thudded loudly in her chest.

"I'll go and see if I can find someone," her mother said, climbing out of the car. "Coming, Jess?"

"No, I think I'll stay here in the yard," Jess squeaked. "I don't want to miss the horsebox."

"All right." Her mother smiled. "Now, it's Jasper Carlisle I'm looking for, isn't it?"

"Yes, or Amy Watkins," Jess said.

Jess had an agonising wait in the stable yard. She wished she'd asked Rosie to come with her, but Rosie was riding at Sandy Lane this afternoon. They all would be. Alex, Kate, Charlie, Tom and Izzy would all be going out on the 11 o'clock hack. Nick would probably be taking it. On any normal Saturday Jess would have been there too. But then, this wasn't any normal Saturday.

"Hi, I'm Camilla. Do you need any help?" a strident voice rang in Jess's ears.

Jess found herself face to face with the blonde rider of the palomino pony, closely followed by a gaggle of three girls. None of them seemed to recognise Jess from their clifftop encounter.

"I'm waiting for my pony, actually," Jess replied quickly. "I'm going to stable it here."

"Another pony? Brilliant. What's it like?" Camilla asked quickly. "Is it fast?"

"Um…" Jess paused. She looked hopelessly at Camilla's beautifully polished riding kit, her perfect hair, her prettily arrogant face, and took a deep breath. "I don't know yet. I won it in a competition."

"Oh, so you're the competition winner," Camilla crowed. "Did you hear that, everyone? This girl's won our competition pony."

Jess squirmed in her shoes and reddened.

"Well, if you need any advice on riding, you're more than welcome to come to me," Camilla offered. "I've had my own pony for ages. He's called Apollo."

Jess gritted her teeth and swallowed hard. "Thanks," she said as graciously as she could bear. Just then, her mother appeared.

"I've had a chat to Amy," she said. "And I've met a few other girls. They all seem very nice. I see you've made a new friend already," she added, looking at Camilla. "Hello, I'm Jess's mum."

Camilla smiled sweetly. "Pleased to meet you. If there's anything Jess needs to know about Rychester, she can always ask me."

"Well that's very kind of you," Jess's mum said.

"OK Jess? Feeling excited?" Amy called as she joined them in the stable yard.

"Hello Amy." Jess smiled. "I'm kind of nervous I suppose –" She stopped as the roar of a motor cut through the cold morning air and a horsebox pulled into Rychester's drive. At last!

The driver jumped down from the cab.

"One pony care of Blackford's," he announced. He headed round to the back of the box, slid back the bolts and lowered the ramp.

Jess hardly dared to breathe. Everyone clamoured to get a glimpse of the pony.

Just then, a red car crunched into the yard.

"Which one's Jess?" a woman asked, jumping out.

"I am," Jess said, suddenly shy.

"Jess, I'm Penny Webster from the *Daily Advertiser* and this is our photographer, Bob," she said, indicating a man by her side. "Is this your mother? Hello Mrs. Adams…nice to meet you."

Before she could say any more, Amy's voice rang out, "Stand back, you lot. The pony's coming down the ramp."

And there at last was Jess's pony, stepping lightly from the box. She was small, about 13 hands. A beautiful, dainty grey mare with large, dark eyes. She sniffed the air with quivering nostrils and looked around the yard inquisitively. She seemed to take everything in. Then she gave a gentle whinny.

Immediately, Jess approached her. She held out her hand and placed it firmly on the pony's velvety nose. "Hello there," she said.

The pony sniffed cautiously at Jess and nuzzled into her shoulder, nibbling gently at her jacket.

"Like her?" Penny Webster smiled across at Jess.

"Yes, oh yes," Jess breathed.

"Hmm, not bad at all." Camilla's voice rang loud and clear. "I bet she's an excellent jumper too. I'll have a closer look later. I'm off on a hack now. I presume our ponies are tacked up, Amy?"

And then she left, followed closely by her friends.

"She's brilliant, Jess," Amy said brightly, as if to make up for the other girls' abrupt departure. "We'll get her settled in no time."

"She does look lovely," Jess's mother agreed. "What are you going to call her, Jess?"

"I expect she's already got a name," Amy said, leafing through the pony's documents that the driver had handed to her. "I'm sure you could change it if you wanted to though. Ah, here we go, it's Skylark."

"Skylark," Jess said softly. "It's perfect."

"Well here's to Skylark and Jess," Penny cried. "Now, we need some photos. Jasper Carlisle really ought to be here. After all, it is his stables, and it was his company that sponsored the competition."

Jasper Carlisle owned Vrai Vert Cosmetics as well as Rychester? It was the first Jess had heard of it. No wonder the competition organizers had been so adamant she had to keep the pony at Rychester...

"I'm afraid I don't know where Jasper's got to," Amy said.

"Well, we'll take a couple of photos of Jess and the pony anyway," Penny decided.

Jess nestled in close to her new pony and beamed as Bob began to snap away. "That's great," he said. "You look very happy, Jess."

"I am," Jess replied. "Happier than ever."

"How about a shot with Mum too?" Penny suggested.

Jess's mother lifted a tentative hand to Skylark's neck and smiled at her daughter. Bob raised his camera for the picture.

At that moment, a shiny green Range Rover came roaring up the drive. Skylark started, but Jess kept a steadying hand on the lead rein. Everyone stared as the car door swung open and a man in a suit climbed out. He was tall, with blond hair neatly slicked back. Stretching out his hand, he strode towards them.

"Hi, everyone," he cried. "Apologies for being late. My meeting overran. No rest for the wicked, eh? Even on a Saturday. I hope I haven't missed all the excitement. Now, where's our lucky winner?"

Amy put a hand on Jess's shoulder. "Jess," she said, "meet Jasper Carlisle, owner of Rychester Stables and boss of Vrai Vert Cosmetics. Jasper, this is Jess Adams, lucky owner of the new pony."

Jasper beamed at Jess. "Excellent," he said. "I hope the pony is to your liking." And then, before Jess could reply, Jasper turned to Penny. "Let's have some photos then. We'll turn this way so we can get the Rychester sign in the background."

He smiled at Jess again. "Welcome to Rychester, Jess. The finest stables in the county!"

Chapter 7

Jump Disaster

There were many more photos after that. By the time Jasper was satisfied, Skylark was twitching with impatience and Jess felt as though her smile was stuck to her face.

"Thank goodness that's over," Jess's mother whispered as Penny drove off. "Jasper Carlisle's a force to be reckoned with!"

"I didn't realise that Vrai Vert Cosmetics and Rychester Stables were owned by the same person," Jess whispered back as she watched Jasper Carlisle disappear into the office.

"Oh, Jasper Carlisle's a renowned businessman," her mother said. "I suppose he must be keen on animals too. This lovely stables, and his cosmetics are very natural – no animal testing, I believe. Maybe you'll be able to get me some free samples, Jess? I love their Mango Miracle Shampoo."

"Honestly, Mum!" Jess groaned. "I've got more important things to think about. Like getting Skylark settled for starters."

"Yes, I suppose I should let you two get to know each other," her mother said, glancing at her watch. "Shall I come back and pick you up in two hours?"

"Thanks, Mum, that would be perfect," Jess replied. "Bye."

Amy saw Jess on her own with Skylark and hurried across.

"I'll take you to Skylark's stable now, show you where you can keep her things and explain a bit about the routine here," she offered. "Then maybe you could try riding her in the indoor school? It's warm and quiet and you can get used to each other."

"Oh yes!" Jess's eyes shone with delight. She still couldn't believe that Skylark was hers...to ride whenever she wanted.

Half an hour later, tacked and mounted, Skylark circled the indoor school. Jess pushed her gently through her paces, from a walk to a rising trot to a collected canter. To her delight, the pony was responsive and alert. Her rhythm was fluid and she even changed pace effortlessly. She really was a dream to ride.

"You've got a lovely rhythm there, Jess," Amy called from the side of the school.

"It's all Skylark," Jess said. "She knows just what to do."

"You're a good rider too, Jess. It's not just the horse," a male voice boomed across the school. "There's no room for modest riders in my stables."

Jess brought Skylark to a halt and looked around to see Jasper Carlisle, leaning against the rail and watching her closely. Jess blushed with pride.

Had Nick ever paid her a compliment like that?

Not that she could remember.

Jasper went on. "You might think about using a stick on her. She's a bit slow around the corners. Still, she's got spirit. Why don't you try her over a few jumps?"

"I'll put the poles out," Amy volunteered.

"Poles?" Jasper laughed. "That's far too tame. Try her on the four footers in the outdoor field."

Did Jasper really mean four foot jumps? Jess tingled nervously.

"Hang on a minute." Amy's voice was steady but concerned. "Jess has only just got this pony, Jasper. And Skylark's probably tired with everything that's happened today. She really needs rest. Besides, the ground outside is still very hard..."

Jess knew Amy was right, but Jasper wasn't having any of it. "Nonsense, she'll be fine," he said. "And I'm sure Jess can get the pony round the course."

Jess looked from one face to the other.

"We could just try one," she volunteered, anxious to please.

Amy gave a deep sigh. "Don't feel you have to do everything today, Jess. She'll still be here tomorrow."

"Follow me," Jasper said.

He led the way out of the covered arena and into a white fenced enclosure. A course of ten huge jumps stood in the afternoon light. Skylark shifted and danced on the spot. Jess looked at Amy's quietly troubled face. *I can't back out now*, Jess thought.

"Come on, Jess, you don't need to do the whole course," Jasper called out. "Just take her over the parallel bars and the brush. Let's see what this little beauty can do."

Jess turned Skylark determinedly towards the first parallel and shortened the reins. Skylark's step was light and quick as Jess leaned forward in the saddle and urged her on. Now they were approaching the first parallel, steady, not too fast. Skylark's hooves thudded over the hard ground and Jess counted her point of take-off. One, two, three and they were soaring through the air. Then it was on to the next parallel. They sailed over that with space to spare and Jess couldn't help grinning madly.

Jasper was right. Skylark was a superb jumper. What's more, she really seemed to be enjoying herself, flicking her tail playfully and giving little dancing, kicking steps.

Jess was enjoying herself too. The feeling was marvellous. Now they only had the brush left. Jess turned Skylark swiftly and they pounded towards it. Within seconds they were suspended in mid-air and Jess's spirits soared with delight.

After that everything seemed to happen in slow-motion. Skylark's forelegs met the ground and hit a patch of frozen ground directly at landing point. There was nothing to grip on to and her legs splayed out in front of her while her hind legs followed. Jess was thrown back onto the ground. Ahead of her, Skylark was lying lifeless where she had fallen.

"No!" Jess screamed, scrambling to her feet.

Simultaneously, both she and Amy rushed over to Skylark. The pony's flanks were heaving and she was panting heavily. Suddenly, with a supreme effort, she raised her head and stumbled her way up to a standing position.

"Skylark," Jess cried.

"Stand back." Jasper's voice was stern, but he looked worried. "She just seems a bit winded that's all," he said briefly. "Amy, bring her back to her stable and get her untacked."

"No...let me!" Jess cried in anguish.

Jasper put his hands up in surprise. "Fair enough," he said. "Amy, call the vet, just to be on the safe side. I want this pony seen quickly. Her picture and Rychester will be all over the *Daily Advertiser* tomorrow. We can't let anything happen to her." And with that, he marched off.

Jess was tense with worry. How could she have been so stupid. "Skylark will be all right, won't she?" Jess asked Amy fearfully.

"She'll be fine." Amy's voice was soothing. "Come on, let's get her to her stable."

Chapter 8

Things Get Better

"She'll need total rest for three days. It's just a nasty knock to the knees," the vet said, smiling kindly. She snapped her bag shut and crunched across the gravel to her car.

Jess turned back to Skylark's stable, flung her arms around the little pony's neck and buried her face into the soft mane. "Everything's going to be all right, Skylark," she said, full of remorse.

"Is everything OK?" came Camilla's now familiar voice. Jess groaned inwardly. But strangely, Camilla was being nice. "I heard about the accident," she continued. "It was bad luck. Daddy said you and Skylark were jumping well."

"Daddy?" Jess repeated the words slowly.

"Yes," Camilla said. "He was watching you."

"You mean…Jasper Carlisle is your father?"

"Yes, silly," Camilla laughed. "I'm Camilla Carlisle. Surely Amy must have told you."

"No," Jess said slowly. "She didn't."

"Well that was very slack of her. Anyway, I'm just about to take Apollo out for a gallop along the coast. Why don't you come with me?"

"But – Skylark." Jess indicated her pony. "I can't ride her for at least three days."

Camilla gave an impatient toss of her head. "Honestly, Jess, there's nothing wrong with her."

"The vet said she had to rest. I'm not going to risk it." Jess was quiet but firm.

Camilla pursed her lips and raised her eyebrows. "Well if you feel like that," she said at last. "I'll get Amy to tack up Dido instead. She's not being ridden at the moment."

"No thanks, I'd better stay and look after Skylark."

"Oh come on, Jess," Camilla said. "Don't be so feeble. It'll be fun. And Skylark will be fine here. Amy'll keep an eye on her."

Jess looked from Skylark to Camilla. She was furious that Camilla had called her feeble. She'd show her. Besides, it was a marvellous day for a ride.

"All right," she said finally. "But I'll tack up Dido."

Camilla shrugged. "Amy's supposed to do that kind of stuff. It's what she's paid for."

"It's what I'm used to," Jess said firmly.

"Suit yourself." Camilla headed off to find Apollo.

Jess turned to Skylark again. "I'll be back soon," she promised, checking the pony's haynet was full. "You take it easy here. It won't be long before we're riding together again."

Mounted on Dido, Jess met up with Camilla in the yard.

"All ready?" Camilla called over her shoulder. "Let's go."

She walked Apollo a little way in front of Jess and

Dido as they made their way out of the stables and along the country lanes.

Jess tried to adjust herself to Dido's rhythm and settle into the saddle. She was nervous about riding a new pony, especially one as impressive as Dido. Seeing the nonchalant way Camilla rode Apollo didn't help. The palomino was skittish, pirouetting and skipping along the road, spooking at every moving twig. But Camilla didn't seem bothered at all. She controlled the nervous pony with offhand grace. Her apparent ease helped to calm Jess, and soon she began to enjoy Dido's regular pace. As they turned the ponies into a field, Jess brought Dido level with Apollo.

"We're heading towards my stables," she told Camilla. "I mean, the stables I used to ride at – Sandy Lane."

"Never heard of it." Camilla shrugged.

"Well it's a lot smaller than Rychester," Jess said. "But it's a lovely place."

"I'll take your word for it." Camilla smirked.

"Of course nowhere could be as great as Rychester. It was my love of horses that inspired Daddy to set it up. He's a businessman really, but he adores animals and with the profits from his cosmetics company he started Rychester. Now he's got a stable full of winning horses!"

"There are some lovely horses at Rychester," Jess agreed with a slight pang of envy. Fancy having a dad who was willing to set up a riding stables just because his daughter loved horses.

"We only have the best, Jess." Camilla flashed a wide grin. "And now we've got Skylark too. She's going to do really well for Rychester, you just see if she doesn't. Come on, let's gallop!"

And with that Camilla turned Apollo to the open grass and spurred him on with her heels. In the next moment they had raced the length of the field. Jess was so astonished at this abrupt departure that she wasn't able to check Dido, who danced excitedly beneath her and then was off, charging after Apollo like a streak of lightning.

The sheer speed gave Jess such a thrill. In no time, she and Dido had crossed the field too. Jess felt breathless and elated.

"That was brilliant, wasn't it?" Camilla cried. "Bet I surprised you."

Jess could only smile back and nod.

The first thing Jess did after the ride was run to check on Skylark. Her heart sank when she saw Jasper leaning against the pony's door. Had something awful happened? Then she saw that he was talking to Penny Webster from the *Daily Advertiser*. What was she doing back so soon? Skylark stood looking out over her stable door.

"Is everything all right?" Jess asked anxiously, nodding at Skylark.

"Absolutely," Jasper replied quickly. "Penny and I were just sorting out a bit more publicity for you and this pony. Just a few informal pictures."

"Along with the rest of the team." Penny smiled.

"Team? What team?" Jess was puzzled.

"I'll ring you in the week, Jasper." Penny turned

to go. "Oh, and look out for Tuesday's *Daily Advertiser*," she said to Jess as she went. "You'll be on the second page."

Jasper turned to Jess. "I didn't tell Penny about Skylark's little accident," he said. "Didn't see much point really, since the vet said she'd be better in a day or two. Anyway there's something more important I want to discuss with you."

Jess wondered what could be more important than Skylark's health.

"That team Penny mentioned," Jasper explained. "It's for the Ash Hill show. I'm relying on you and Skylark to do well in the Open Jumping. Your score would count towards a team medal for Rychester. We need five riders. Camilla will be entering with three of our regulars."

"The Ash Hill show?" Jess echoed, her heart beating faster. "But do you think I'll be ready? I've hardly ridden Skylark yet. I wanted to take things slowly, get to know her first."

"That's very admirable, Jess," Jasper said. "But

I think you're being overcautious. You and Skylark will be fine. I've seen you ride. Ash Hill's a month and a half away after all, and Skylark has had excellent training. She should do well for us. And so will you – with some Rychester tuition."

"But I can't afford lessons…"

"Don't worry," Jasper said, holding his hand up in the air. "I'll take care of all that. But don't forget: I pay for the best and I expect the best."

And that, it seemed, was that. Jasper walked away, leaving Jess reeling with excitement and shock.

"Everything's happening so quickly, Skylark," she whispered into the pony's ear. "Not so long ago having my own pony was just a dream and I had to muck out in return for my rides. Now I've got you, I'm part of this smart stables and I'm going to jump at Ash Hill!"

Jess was interrupted again by Camilla's voice. "Jess, would you like to come and have some tea at my house? I want to show you something."

Jess couldn't really say no. She gave Skylark a last

pat and hurried out of the stable.

"Come on," Camilla said, leading Jess to the grand, gabled house. It was a far cry from Jess's rather shabby cottage. Jess walked through the front door and looked around in awe at the cool, marbled entrance hall.

"Is that you, Camilla darling?" A shrill voice echoed into the hallway and soon a taller version of Camilla, dressed in smart pale trousers and a long jacket, emerged in the hallway.

"Hi Mum, we're starving," Camilla announced.

"Oh, are you?" Camilla's mother seemed perplexed. "I'm just off out, darling. You'll have to forage in the kitchen I'm afraid."

"OK," Camilla replied. "This is Jess by the way. She won the pony, you know, Dad's competition."

"How lovely." Camilla's mother smiled with brief distraction at Jess. "See you later, darlings," she said, and she was gone.

"This way," Camilla said to Jess.

She led Jess into a vast kitchen. Stainless steel

cupboards lined the walls, spotless and gleaming. Camilla delved into one of them and drew out a tin. "Chocolate biscuits," she announced triumphantly. "We'll take these up to my room."

Camilla marched up the stairs and down a long corridor, past several closed doors. Finally she stopped outside one of them.

"Here we are," she said, turning the handle and Jess followed her in.

Camilla's room was decidedly pink. The walls were painted with hundreds of tiny stars and a four poster bed swathed in pink muslin stood in the middle of the room. Pink and white curtains draped the windows and the floor was covered with a thick pink carpet. Shelves around the room were lined with bottles of creams and lotions, all with the distinctive green Vrai Vert logo.

"I've got hundreds of bottles of the stuff." Camilla laughed, seeing Jess looking at the shelves. "Here, take some." And she thrust a wicker basket of Vrai Vert goodies into her hands.

"Um, thanks," Jess mumbled. At least her mother would be pleased.

"What do you think?" Camilla said, indicating the room.

"Erm...lovely," said Jess. "You must like pink."

"Not especially," Camilla replied in an offhand way. "Mummy chose it all, then had it photographed by some design magazine."

This sounded rather glamorous to Jess, but Camilla didn't seem to think so.

"Come and look at these," said Camilla, darting across the room to a small alcove. Inside there was a glass cabinet displaying lines of cups, trophies and rosettes. Camilla Carlisle, First, New Benningdon Horse Trials, one trophy inscription read. Dressage First Place, Southdown Show, read another. First Prize, Colcott Cross Country Team Chase, a third was engraved.

"Wow." Jess was suitably impressed.

"These are only some of the trophies of course," Camilla declared. "Daddy's got the main ones displayed downstairs. And the Ash Hill Team Event will soon be joining them."

"Did you win all these with Apollo?" Jess asked, picturing Camilla and her beautiful palomino pony jumping effortlessly at show after show.

"Some of them," Camilla said. "But I've won on other horses too. Daddy only buys the best horses. Now Rychester has got Skylark too. She's going to win loads of prizes for us."

"Don't forget she's my pony," Jess said, pointedly, "not Rychester's."

"Of course she is, silly." Camilla flashed her a quick smile, and after the briefest of pauses spoke again. "Look, Jess," she said, "I hope you don't think me rude, but those jods you're wearing have seen better days."

Jess felt embarrassed as she looked down at her scruffy, old jodhpurs. She couldn't even remember how long she'd had them.

"I'm sure you'll be buying some soon," Camilla continued lightly, "but Mummy's just bought me two new pairs so would you like my old ones?"

She fished around in the bottom of a wardrobe and produced what to Jess looked like a brand-new pair of beige jodhpurs.

"They're about your size I think," Camilla said. "I was only going to throw them out."

"Well, if you're sure…" Jess was hesitant but she wasn't proud. It was obvious that Camilla's parents could easily afford new clothes and that Camilla would have no hesitation in discarding anything she'd lost interest in. Jess accepted the jodhpurs graciously and Camilla smiled broadly.

"You can wear them when you ride Skylark again," she said. "It won't be long now. And then we'll really have fun. We're going to have some brilliant hacks together."

Her enthusiasm made Jess grin too. "We *will* have fun," she said to herself. "And I've got my very own pony to ride. Brilliant!"

Chapter 9

Jess Moves On

Jess sat at the kitchen table, chatting as her mother made supper. For what must have been the fifteenth time that day, Jess began to talk about Rychester again.

"Mrs. Carlisle had Camilla's room photographed for a magazine," she said. "And Camilla's dad set up Rychester Riding Stables just for Camilla. Isn't that amazing?"

"Fascinating, Jess," her mother said, wearily. Jess could see her mother looked run-down. Her ancient leggings and baggy old sweater didn't help matters.

"Now, what can I do for your supper, Jess? You won't want spaghetti Bolognese like the rest of us."

"No, sorry Mum," Jess said. She knew that not eating meat caused her mother extra work. But no matter how many times she said she'd just have the vegetables, or make herself a sandwich, her mother would always go out of her way to make her something else.

"You're a growing girl, Jess," she would say. "You can't survive on sandwiches."

Jess said she was happy with just pasta and cheese, then let her thoughts drift back to Rychester. The more time she spent there, the more she liked it. Amy was encouraging and Camilla had really taken her under her wing. And Skylark – well, Skylark was the most wonderful pony in the world.

Jess was still haunted by the accident that first day, but at least Skylark was better now. Jasper had been right, there was no point in telling people what had gone on. Jess's mum and dad would only worry. And Jess simply couldn't tell Rosie. She didn't want to fuel Rosie's doubts about Rychester. In fact, she'd hardly spoken to Rosie all week...

They had both been busy. Rosie was involved in netball trials after school, and Jess had been at Rychester every evening. Jess's phone rang, and she felt a pang of guilt when she saw Rosie's name.

"Rosie! I was just thinking of you."

"Are you around at the weekend?" Rosie asked. "There's a beach ride going out from Sandy Lane. You could bring Skylark."

"Um..." Jess hesitated. The vet had said Skylark was OK to ride, but Jess didn't want to push it. She'd been planning to ride her quietly in the indoor school, under Amy's supervision. "I don't think I can, Rosie," she said. "I think I should get to know her a bit more before I take her out on a hack."

"Fair enough." Rosie's voice was quiet but understanding. "I saw another picture of you in the paper by the way. Lovely cheesy grin!"

"What, me or Skylark?" Jess laughed now.

"You of course," Rosie chortled. "Skylark looks

beautiful. In black and white anyway."

"She is beautiful, Rosie," Jess said. "And you will see her soon, I promise."

"I can't wait," Rosie replied eagerly. "I was beginning to think you'd forgotten all about your old Sandy Lane mates. Are you a Rychester girl now? Posh clothes, daring riding?"

"Oh Rychester's not so bad," Jess said quickly. "In fact, it's better than I expected… You should see it, Rosie." Jess's voice rose with excitement. "The loose boxes are huge, and really smart. That girl we saw on the clifftop ride, the one with the palomino pony, she's Camilla Carlisle, the daughter of Rychester's owner, Jasper. She seemed really snooty at first, but she's all right underneath. And the horses are wonderful. There's Apollo, and Dido, and Skylark of course." Jess paused for breath. "And I'm riding at Ash Hill too, for Rychester. Jasper Carlisle reckons Skylark's going to be brilliant at jumping. She's really responsive to ride."

"Well it all sounds perfect," Rosie said brightly.

"What's the news at Sandy Lane?" Jess asked quickly, realising she'd just been gabbling about herself. "Am I missing anything?"

"Not really," Rosie said. "Nick's been in a bad mood because his flu's come back and lots of people seem to be cancelling rides. I'm definitely jumping Pepper at the Ash Hill Show in the Open Jumping…"

Jess struggled to focus on Rosie's chatter. She was wondering what Skylark was doing now. Had Amy checked her for the night? When would Jess see her next? Where would she take her for a ride?

"Jess," Rosie was calling, "Jess are you there?"

"Yes," Jess said quickly. Rosie's hurt silence hung in the air. "It sounds like things are pretty busy then," Jess added.

"I guess so." Rosie's voice was quiet and Jess felt wretched for not paying her more attention. "I have to go," she lied miserably. "My mum's calling me."

Chapter 10

Friends Old and New

It was a busy two weeks for Jess. There was school and homework and jobs around the house to fit in, but every evening, as soon as she was free, she would cycle the twenty minutes to Rychester to spend time with Skylark. At the end of the first week, she had ridden her pony at last.

"You've been wise to wait," Amy told her encouragingly.

To Jess's delight, there seemed to be no lasting damage to the pony's knees. One evening there was another publicity photo session with the *Daily*

Advertiser, the Rychester Stables sign prominently displayed in the background.

"Let's show them a fit and eager pony, and a healthy, happy rider," Jasper had urged Jess, shoving a bottle of New Improved Mango Miracle Shampoo into her hand as she smiled broadly for the camera.

Camilla was often at the stables in the evening too. She would ride Apollo in the indoor school, training him for the Ash Hill show. Jess watched them with admiration. Apollo cleared the jumps effortlessly, with a proud flick of his tail. Jess noticed that Camilla kept him on a very tight rein, which caused the palomino pony to skip and toss his head. But the more Apollo pirouetted, the tighter Camilla sat to the saddle. She didn't flinch or move a muscle.

After all the lessons in the indoor school during the week, Jess was looking forward to a relaxing hack in the open air. She swung herself up into Skylark's saddle and gathered up the reins.

"Give Skylark a good run now." Jasper's voice was brisk and efficient. "She needs the exercise."

"Yes," Jess replied eagerly, "but I'm not going to take any risks."

"Absolutely," Jasper said. "You need to save yourselves for the Ash Hill Show. The *Daily Advertiser* will be following your progress with interest, so you'd better come back with a rosette. Now go on, enjoy the hack."

He gave Skylark a slap on the rump and the little pony lurched forward. Jess quickly put a steadying hand on the front of the saddle. Jasper's words made Jess feel uneasy, bullied almost. But he was relying on her and that made her feel important.

"We'll have to train really hard, Skylark," she whispered to her pony. "But we can do it."

As she walked on to where Camilla and Apollo were waiting, a thought occurred to her. "Camilla, do you want to do some training for Rychester tonight?" she asked her new friend. "Apollo's quite fearless around the ring. It might be good for Skylark to follow him."

Camilla glanced at her impatiently. "Tonight?

Sorry, Jess, I'm busy. Lucy and Samantha are coming round for supper. Now hurry up, slow coach, we've been waiting ages for you!"

Jess felt strangely deflated that she hadn't been included in Camilla's plans, but at least she was out riding with the girls now.

Samantha rode her brown pony, Amber, Lucy was on Dido, and Allison was riding Rychester's Jackdaw. These were the same girls who had ridden with Camilla that day on the clifftops.

It's hardly surprising that they didn't recognise me, Jess thought. Back then she was riding shaggy little Minstrel in her scruffy old anorak. Now she was riding a beautifully turned-out pony, wearing Camilla's smart jods and had even brushed her hair. Jess had taken to washing her hair with Camilla's shampoo, which really did make it smell nice.

"So you're jumping Skylark at Ash Hill?" Samantha called across.

"Yes," Jess replied. "If we're ready."

"You'll be ready," Camilla joined in. "Apollo's

bound to win tons of stuff. You can watch me and see how it's done."

"Honestly, Camilla," Allison retorted. "You're such a show-off. All five of us are entered for Ash Hill. Together we've got a good chance of winning the team medal."

Camilla smiled gleefully. "That's true, Allison, so of course you might win something," she conceded. "But it'll be me and Apollo galloping away with the Open Jumping trophy."

"Show us how you're going to do it then, Cam." Allison's voice was excited as they turned the ponies off the lane and into a stubble field. "See those logs over there?"

She pointed to the edge of the field where a pile of timber was stacked toweringly high. Sharp twigs and coarse brush stuck out from the log pile, and the whole construction looked very precarious. "Bet you can't jump that."

Camilla followed her gaze and laughed scornfully. "That's child's play!" she crowed. "But I bet you lot will be too chicken to follow me."

"Oo, a dare!" Allison cried. "I'll be right behind you, Camilla."

"Me too!" said Lucy.

"Count me in then," Samantha added.

"What about you, Jess?" Camilla turned Apollo to face Skylark. "Fancy a challenge?"

Jess looked at the precarious pile of wood. It was very high. One knock from a pony's hoof and the whole lot would come crashing down dangerously. There was another problem too. The point of take-off for the jump was clear enough, but the landing point wasn't visible and there was a wood immediately behind. It was crazy...mad. Jess shifted uncomfortably in the saddle. They were all looking at her.

"Scared?" Allison sneered.

"It's just a stupid thing to do," Jess said fiercely.

"Yep, she's scared," Allison cried triumphantly.

"No she's not," Camilla said, looking directly at Jess. "She'll follow us. Won't you, Jess?" And before

Jess could say anything, Camilla turned Apollo sharply and kicked him into a gallop across the field.

Jess could hardly watch as they approached the timber pile at breakneck speed. Surely they would crash straight into it. At the very last moment, Camilla must have checked Apollo because he seemed to stop still in mid-gallop. And then, like a Harrier Jump Jet taking off, he sprang over the logs with centimetres to spare. On landing, Camilla pulled him up sharply and the horse turned on the spot before stopping directly at the edge of the forest. Camilla gave a triumphant wave and beckoned the rest of the ride to follow.

"Come on, Jess, live a little," Samantha called over her shoulder.

Jess took a deep breath and watched them. Now Samantha was clear, and Lucy too. Skylark pulled at the reins, pawing at the ground and walking in impatient circles. The air was crisp and clear and suddenly Jess felt a surge of confidence. Skylark was just as good as any of those ponies…better even.

Suddenly the jump looked exciting and inviting.

As Allison pushed Jackdaw safely over the timber, Jess's mind was made up. Skylark didn't need to be told a second time to gallop, and in an instant the little grey pony was flying across the ground. Jess's spirits soared with every step.

And now the timber pile loomed nearer, even larger than Jess had anticipated. Keeping a firm but light hold of the reins she focused straight ahead, right between Skylark's alert ears. She could just make out the rest of the ride, waiting for her on the other side of the jump. As she drew near to her point of take-off, they seemed to multiply into lots of ponies and riders.

Focus on the jump, Jess thought, and with a swift kick she urged Skylark on. Soon they were soaring lightly through the air. When they landed – a little shakily, but clear – Jess's momentary feeling of elation gave way to blind panic as she saw she was hurtling straight for a group of horses.

"Look out!" a familiar voice cried.

At the last minute, Jess gave an almighty tug on Skylark's reins and swung the surprised pony to the left, just avoiding a collision.

"Jess!" came the same voice. "What on earth do you think you're playing at? You could have killed someone."

Tom Buchanan sat looking down at her from Chancey. He shook his head slowly.

"Tom!" Jess gasped. Of course, it was the 2 o'clock Sandy Lane hack.

"You obviously didn't see us riding out of the woods," Tom continued, his voice tight with anger. "There could have been a really nasty accident."

"I…" Jess began, but she was lost for words. It was Camilla who jumped to her rescue.

"Oh shut up, Grandad," she sneered at Tom. "This is a fantastic jump and Jess cleared it beautifully."

Samantha, Lucy and Allison laughed heartily. Tom went puce with rage and shot Jess a filthy look. Jess squirmed with embarrassment and stared at the ground. She so desperately wanted to apologise, but

Tom was already walking Chancey on in silent fury.

Then suddenly Rosie was riding towards her, on the back of dear old Pepper.

"I don't think much of your new friends, Jess," she whispered across, "but you did clear that jump spectacularly. I'd never have had the nerve. So this is Skylark?" she went on. "She's beautiful."

Suddenly Jess missed Sandy Lane very much. Most of all she missed being with Rosie.

"Why don't I bring Skylark over to Sandy Lane this evening?" she suggested eagerly. "You could ride her then."

"That would have been lovely." Rosie shrugged apologetically. "But I'm going to the cinema with Izzy tonight."

Jess gave a small smile and tried to sound cheerful. She couldn't help feeling a tiny bit jealous. "Well, maybe another time," she said.

"I'd like that," Rosie said, as she walked on with the Sandy Lane riders.

Jess watched her go, until Camilla's strident voice

rang in her ears. "Come on, Jess," she urged. "Let's get back to some proper riding."

At the end of the hour, the Rychester ride wound its way back to the stables. They'd had several good gallops and jumped some small logs, but they were still full of the success of clearing the timber pile.

"Just wait till we get to Ash Hill," Camilla cried. "We'll be the best showjumpers they've ever seen."

Jess said very little. Across the yard, she saw Amy talking urgently to someone by Skylark's box.

"I couldn't really say," Amy was saying. "It's just what my cousin Barry tells me really."

"Well, let me know if you hear anything else," a voice replied. "Keep an eye on Jasper perhaps."

Then Amy shifted her position and Jess saw it was the journalist Penny Webster she was talking to.

"Jess, there you are," said Penny. "I was just asking Amy where I might find you."

"Oh," Jess said, hoping Penny wasn't after any more photos.

"I came by to find out how you were getting on

with Skylark," Penny said. "Are you pleased with your prize pony?"

"Oh yes." Jess's hesitance gave way to eager enthusiasm. "She's just brilliant. Thanks."

"Well she looks lovely," Penny said, giving Skylark a pat.

"Do you want me to untack her?" Amy asked.

"No of course not." Jess shook her head. "I want to do it myself, but thanks anyway."

"Good for you." Amy smiled. "I'd better go and see what state Camilla's left poor Apollo in."

"I'll be in touch," Penny called to Amy before turning back to Jess. "Lovely to see you, Jess. Now I must dash." And with a quick wave she was gone.

"That was a flying visit," Jess said to Skylark. "Come on now, let's get this saddle off."

Chapter 11

The Competition Looms

"So how's this pony of yours, Jess? Fed up with it yet?" Jess's father poked a log around the fire-grate and a cosy glow filled the small sitting room.

"Don't be silly, Dad." Jess laughed, pulling her boots on. "I'll never get fed up with Skylark."

"Well, I must say, you're organizing everything very well, taking care of the pony and keeping up with your school work too. I admire your dedication."

Jess smiled. It was tempting to join him by the fireside and read her new pony book, but Skylark was waiting for her and Ash Hill was looming. She said goodbye to her dad and battled her bicycle down the garden path against the March wind.

Jasper had hired Martin Jennings, ex-Olympic riding star, to train the Ash Hill entrants, all at his own expense. "He'll get you jumping like winners," Jasper had announced.

The jumping lessons were gruelling, but Jess was doing well and Martin Jennings seemed pleased with her progress.

This Saturday morning, Jasper stood watching next to Martin. Lucy had just knocked two fences down on Dido, but Jess, concentrating hard, thundered clear around the course. She would have been elated, but Jasper put a damper on things.

"That was far too hesitant," he said. "Push her straight at the jump. Show her who's boss."

Jess swallowed hard and patted Skylark.

Next it was Allison on Jackdaw.

"Too slow!" Jasper cried. "You'll lose us vital marks if you don't step up the pace."

Allison went red and trotted Jackdaw to the far

side of the ring. Then came Samantha on Amber. They did all right until the final wall, which Amber just caught with her rear hoof.

Jasper's reaction was immediate and unforgiving. "You lost concentration, Samantha!" he shouted. "You relaxed and it cost you four faults. That's four faults I don't want to see at Ash Hill. Understood?"

Samantha hung her head and mumbled a "yes".

Jess winced inwardly and gave her a sympathetic glance. One fence down wasn't exactly a disaster. But Jasper was a hard taskmaster. He expected nothing less than first place. With Martin's tuition, it was clear they were in with a real chance, but Jasper's demands for perfection were unrealistic. Nick would never be so demanding, Jess found herself thinking.

Now it was Camilla's turn. Jess watched Apollo clear the jumps spectacularly and swiftly.

"Wow, that was a brilliant round, Camilla," Jess called over.

"Well done, Camilla." Martin smiled quickly.

"Much better!" Jasper roared.

Jess was glad when at last the lesson was over. "You jumped very well, Skylark," she whispered as she led the pony back to her stable.

She slipped the bridle off Skylark's nose and hung it on the stable door, then lifted the heavy saddle down from her back. As Jess carried the saddle to the tack room, she whistled softly to herself. She didn't think she could ever get bored with this familiar routine of untacking and settling her pony – her very own pony! She thought of all the other ponies she had looked after, Minstrel and Pepper and Hector and Storm Cloud. Jess paused. Storm Cloud! Since Skylark, Jess had hardly given Storm Cloud another thought.

"Poor Stormy," Jess said to herself. "I wonder if her leg's any better. Maybe I should ride over to Sandy Lane now to see her. I could see Rosie too."

She was about to turn back to Skylark's stable when she heard angry voices coming from the tack room. She didn't want to eavesdrop, but the voices were so loud, she couldn't help hearing snatches of conversation. It was definitely Jasper in there and the other voice sounded like Amy's. But Amy wasn't being her usual calm, restrained self...

"What did you say to the press about me?" Jasper screamed.

"Nothing," Amy spat back. "Why? Do you have something to hide, Jasper?"

Jess thought she heard the door opening and quickly rushed back to Skylark's stable.

"It's a good job we're heading out again," she said to the surprised pony. "Going into the tack room would have been like walking into a lion's den. Come on, let's go and see some old friends of mine."

Half an hour later, Jess and Skylark turned into Sandy Lane. Everything seemed very quiet as she slipped down from the saddle and led Skylark along the row of stables.

Suddenly Jess's heart leapt. There was dear Stormy now, poking her delicate grey nose out of the last stable door. But Storm Cloud was not alone.

Hunched over the door stood Nick Brooks talking softly to the pony.

A snort from Skylark announced Jess's arrival and Storm Cloud whinnied in reply.

"Hello, stranger," Nick said, turning his head round. "Everyone's out on a hack, I'm afraid."

"Oh." Jess felt embarrassed. "It was actually Stormy I wanted to see," she began.

"Well, she's certainly pleased to see you." Nick laughed as Storm Cloud craned her head over the stable door and chewed expectantly at Jess's coat.

"You're in luck, Stormy," said Jess, fishing out a stray sugar lump from the depths of her pocket. "I was saving this for you."

"Better not make this one jealous," Nick said, indicating Skylark. "Is this your prize pony?"

"Um, yes." Jess's pride in Skylark was tinged with shame at not bringing her to see Nick sooner.

"She's lovely." Nick smiled kindly and rubbed Skylark's nose. "And how's Rychester working out?"

Jess didn't know what to say. She thought of Jasper

Carlisle and his short temper. She couldn't imagine him taking time to talk to one of his horses. She thought of Camilla and her superior ways, of the gleamingly clinical stable yard at Rychester, of the fierce argument she had heard earlier.

"Oh, it's brilliant," she said finally.

"Good." Nick smiled down at her. "I'm glad it's working out for you, Jess. Although we all miss you at Sandy Lane of course."

Jess was silent. She hadn't expected to hear that from Nick. *I miss Sandy Lane too!* she wanted to cry out. But she couldn't say that now, not after she had just told Nick how wonderful everything was. Suddenly Jess didn't want to hang about any more. She didn't want to smile brightly and answer the inevitable questions about Rychester that her friends would be bound to ask on returning from their ride.

"I have to go," she said quickly to Nick. "Will you tell everyone I said hello, and I'll see them soon?"

Nick nodded and Jess gave Storm Cloud a pat goodbye. As she walked Skylark along the winding country lanes back to Rychester, she thought about Nick and Stormy, and about Sandy Lane too. Then she thought about Skylark and Rychester.

"I should be the happiest girl in the world," she said to Skylark. "I've got you and we're jumping in a really good competition soon and I'm part of the smartest riding school around. So why do I feel so miserable?" But of course, Skylark didn't reply.

Jess was welcomed into the Rychester yard by a cross-looking Camilla.

"It's a good job you're always so keen on untacking Skylark yourself," Camilla huffed.

"What do you mean?" Jess asked.

"Daddy's gone and sacked Amy."

Chapter 12

Jess Has Doubts

Jess didn't feel as comfortable at Rychester without Amy. Her replacement was a brusque, unhelpful, sour-faced girl called Mel. Jess missed Amy's friendly face and no one knew where she was now.

Meanwhile, lessons for Ash Hill continued apace. Martin Jennings was still training them once a week, with Jasper interfering whenever he wasn't at work. Mel seemed to see it as her role to back Jasper up, so any criticism he doled out felt doubly harsh.

The Ash Hill team were all capable riders but, anxious to get into Jasper's good books, an uneasy feeling of competitiveness had crept its way between them. Only Camilla seemed oblivious to it all. She had inherited her father's obsession with success. All her talk was of Apollo bringing home a load of rosettes for Rychester. Of course Jess hoped to do well too, but Skylark meant so much more to her than just a way to win races.

"I wish you'd get your act together, Jess," Camilla snorted after one particularly bad lesson. Skylark had refused twice and finally run out at the second last fence. "I'm beginning to think you'll be more of a liability than an asset at Ash Hill."

Jess was furious. "Skylark and I would be fine if people like you and your dad would lay off us."

Camilla shrugged in an offhand manner. "If Apollo showed me up like that, I would think about selling him on."

"Selling him on?" Jess gasped in disbelief. "But Camilla, you couldn't part with him, he's perfect."

"The only perfect ponies are prize-winning ponies," Camilla said airily. "That's what Daddy always says and he's right."

That same afternoon, Jess bumped into Jasper in the yard.

"Off for a spot of jumping?" he demanded.

"No. I was going to take Skylark out for a hack." Jess was nervous, but determined. She wouldn't let Jasper bully her.

"I don't think that's such a good idea," Jasper said sternly. "You should be cramming in all the jumping practice you can. Skylark's the only Rychester pony without a rosette, Jess. And there's only room for winners in my stables."

Jess waited for him to smile in jest, but he walked off, deadly serious. She was amazed that anyone could be so heartless. Thank goodness she was off to see Rosie. That would brighten her day.

"Oh Jess, she's a dream to ride." Rosie grinned broadly as she drew Skylark to a halt at the edge of the field.

Jess smiled back from Minstrel's saddle. "She's lovely, isn't she?" Minstrel snorted loudly. "You're lovely too, Minstrel." Jess laughed, patting the skewbald's shaggy neck.

"I wish we could ride out together every evening," said Rosie contentedly.

Riding back with Rosie, Jess felt happy for the first time in ages. She knew she'd have to head back to Rychester soon to stable Skylark, but for now it was as if she'd never left Sandy Lane. It had been excellent to share her new pony with Rosie at last. And it had been comforting to ride Minstrel again, whose familiar gait and steady ways inspired a warm, nostalgic feeling for her old stables.

As they clattered into the yard, Tom gave them a friendly wave. Even Alex and Kate stopped arguing for long enough to greet Jess.

"Skylark's lovely, you lucky thing," Charlie called as he unchained his bike.

Jess tethered Skylark to the yard rail and followed Rosie into Minstrel's stable.

"How are the Ash Hill preparations going at Rychester?" Rosie asked conversationally.

"Oh, everyone's pretty determined," Jess said briskly. She didn't feel like talking about Rychester. She was more interested in Sandy Lane. "What's the news here?" she asked.

"Well, Storm Cloud's still lame, but the vet's coming to check her in the next few days," Rosie began. "And Izzy and I have been practising for Ash Hill together. Pepper and Midnight get on well, so we try to ride together after school, but it's hard to take it too seriously. Izzy's so funny, we always end up laughing. Nick gets cross with us though. He says it's the focused and determined riders who'll do best at Ash Hill. Um, what else?" Rosie slipped off Minstrel's bridle. "Oh yes, there's a little girl just started lessons. Her name's Hannah. She adores Minstrel and has been spoiling him rotten – loading him up with sugar lumps. Minstrel thinks it's brilliant. He's devoted to her."

Rosie chattered away excitedly, and Jess felt a pang of envy. *They're obviously not missing me at all,* she thought.

"Nick's having all his Ash Hill riders round for supper on Friday after school," Rosie continued, "to say thanks for all the extra work we've done – grooming horribly muddy ponies, clearing out leaky stables… Nick says he's really proud of us regulars and, oh –" Rosie stopped short as she caught sight of Jess's mournful expression.

"It's all right, Rosie." Jess gave a little shrug. "I know I'm not a Sandy Lane regular any more. It sounds as if you're all having a lot of fun."

"Well…" Rosie sounded apologetic. "It's been all right. Probably nowhere near as exciting as the things you've been doing. We miss you, Jess. You're the lucky one, having Skylark and being able to keep her at Rychester. I mean, it's top of the range!"

"Nothing but the best for Jasper Carlisle," Jess muttered under her breath.

Chapter 13

Revelations

"Ooh, listen to this," cooed Jess's brother, Jack, reading from his tablet. "'The Ash Hill Show will be officially opened at 11 o'clock by Prunella Goldes, star of the hit television series *Horses For Courses*.' I quite fancy her actually. Think I might come after all."

"You're awful, Jack," Jess snorted in disgust. "Can I have a look?"

"Go on then, just while I grab my stuff," said Jack, handing over the tablet and racing upstairs.

The page Jack was reading was on the *Daily*

Advertiser website, but it was another headline that caught Jess's eye: "Proof of Animal Testing at Lab of Shame, by Penny Webster".

Jess clicked on the link and read the article with mounting horror, as familiar names leapt out and grabbed her by the throat.

Vrai Vert Cosmetics has long prided itself on its cruelty-free beauty products, the article declared. *Brands such as Mango Miracle Shampoo and Essence of Peach Perfume are household names. Now an unnamed source has revealed that animals were routinely used for testing during the redevelopment of the company's bestselling product, recently relaunched as New Improved Mango Miracle Shampoo. Vrai Vert Cosmetics Managing Director, Jasper Carlisle, a local man and owner of the county's renowned Rychester Riding Stables, was unavailable for comment yesterday.*

Jess couldn't read any more. She thought of Amy and Jasper's angry exchange. Was Amy the "unnamed source"? Jess put her head in her hands.

"Everything OK, Jess?" Her mother's voice was

concerned as she came into the room, automatically going to the sofa to straighten the cushions.

Jess closed the web page quickly. The last thing she wanted was for her mother to have doubts about Rychester. What would Jess do without the free stabling for Skylark? But her mother had heard the news already.

"Vrai Vert Cosmetics is in a spot of bother," she said, as if reading Jess's mind.

"I saw. Is it bad news for Rychester?" Jess asked.

"I don't know about the stables," her mother replied slowly. "But if the story's true, Jasper's probably broken some kind of advertising law. The shampoo label clearly says it hasn't been tested on animals. A false claim could be quite serious."

Jess looked horrified. When her phone rang a few moments later, she was still in a daze.

"Jess, have you heard the news?" came Rosie's excited voice. "Jasper Carlisle's been accused of letting animals be used for cruel experiments!"

"Yes," Jess said slowly. "I've just read it."

She thought of the times she had raved about Rychester and bit her tongue with embarrassment. "But we don't know if the story's true yet," Jess added.

Rosie remained silent for a moment, then spoke again, in a carefully controlled way. "You're right, Jess. It might all be some awful mistake. So anyway, have you done that English homework yet? I thought the comprehension was really hard…"

Chapter 14

Dilemma

Rychester Stables was buzzing with the news when Jess arrived there the next morning.

"Daddy's absolutely furious," announced Camilla. "He says he's going to sue that Penny Webster for all the things she said."

"So it's definitely not true?" Jess asked, hopefully.

"Of course it isn't," Camilla scoffed. "Daddy's convinced that Amy concocted the story to get back at him for sacking her. It's not his fault that she was so lazy."

Jess didn't know Amy very well, but she definitely

wasn't lazy. The whole situation didn't make sense.

On her way past the office, Jess heard Jasper's voice. "I'm so sorry Julia feels she no longer wishes to ride here. I can assure you the *Daily Advertiser* is completely mistaken. Perhaps we could work this out over a drink at my house... All right. I'll speak to you soon. Tell Gerald we must get together for that game of golf sometime..."

Jess hurried on to Skylark's box. "We'll just get today's jumping lesson over with," she whispered.

Skylark gave a little snort.

"So, Ash Hill tomorrow..." Jasper was addressing the riders at the end of their lesson. "We've got some serious jumping to do and a trophy to win."

Jess stroked Skylark's nose gently and felt uncomfortable. She still hadn't decided whether she believed the news story or not. And now she couldn't get excited about Ash Hill. She felt empty...hollow.

Jess looked at her other team-mates. None of them had ridden well. Samantha seemed nervous and tense, as if she was already thinking about what would happen if she failed to win anything. Allison was looking sullen and even Lucy was kicking the ground miserably with her heels. Only Camilla appeared unconcerned. She had good reason to feel confident. Then again, Jess wasn't sure what emotions her imperious face was masking.

"We'll meet here tomorrow morning at 7 o'clock sharp," Jasper concluded. "No dawdlers." And with that he turned briskly and was gone.

The others set about searching for Mel to untack their ponies. Jess hung back a little and watched them leave. Rychester wasn't a team at all. There was no warmth or comradeship there. What was she doing with them? In all likelihood, Rychester had been set up with the profits from animal experiments. The thought made Jess feel sick. She couldn't face taking Skylark back to the yard now.

"Let's go for a quiet hack instead," she said. "We can clear our heads, think things through a bit."

They trotted out of the stable yard and down the winding lane. As Jess turned the bend she almost bumped into a girl hurrying along the grass verge.

"Amy!" Jess said in surprise. "What are you doing here?"

"Hello Jess." Amy smiled, startled but friendly. "I'm working at Southdown Stables now. I just came back to pick up some things I'd left in the tack room at Rychester." She held up a bag.

"But Jasper," Jess began slowly. "Did he see you? He's really cross with you, you know."

"Frightened more like," Amy replied grimly. "No, I took a chance while you were having a lesson. I crept in and out quickly. You heard the news then?"

"Yes, we all did," Jess said. She climbed down from the saddle and slipped the reins over Skylark's neck as the pony bent down to graze at the verge. "What's going on, Amy? Is what Penny Webster wrote true? And why did Jasper sack you?"

Amy laughed. "That's a lot of questions, Jess. OK, first of all, whatever you might have heard, Jasper didn't sack me. I resigned. Jasper's way of doing things just made me uncomfortable. He was pushing everyone too hard. He didn't really care about the horses at all. I think that was obvious to everyone. He's just in it for the glory they can bring to him. I couldn't handle his obsession with winning."

Amy paused and Jess was silent. She knew that Amy was speaking the truth. Rychester wasn't the kind of stables Jess had hoped it would be, and that had everything to do with Jasper. He had charmed and flattered her at first, but he had also been bullying and threatening.

"I overheard you and Jasper arguing in the tack room," Jess confessed. "Something about the press."

"Ah yes, the final straw." Amy smiled. "That was all a bit of a coincidence really. My cousin Barry was working as a technician at the Vrai Vert Cosmetics Laboratory. The company were relaunching their Mango Miracle Shampoo and he told me that quite a lot of animal testing had taken place during the new product trials. It's all a bit complicated, but basically it means that Jasper's advertising slogan was a lie."

Amy stopped to draw breath, and Jess waited anxiously for her to start again.

"Anyway, I was so fed up at Rychester that I ended up mentioning it to Penny Webster. Penny's never one to turn down a good story. Surprisingly enough, what Jasper's done isn't actually illegal, but it's the kind of thing that could cause a public outcry and do his company's reputation a lot of damage. So now you know, Jess. It's all true."

"Oh Amy, this is awful," Jess wailed. "I've been looking forward to Ash Hill so much. But now it just feels all wrong – riding for Rychester I mean. What should I do?"

Amy smiled at her sympathetically. "You're the only one who knows the answer to that, Jess," she said gently.

Chapter 15

Nightmare

The day of the Ash Hill Show dawned bright and clear. In contrast, Jess felt tired and gloomy as she cycled towards Rychester shortly after 7 o'clock. She had lain awake all night, churning things over in her mind: her conversation with Amy, Penny's article, Jasper's insistence on winning, the absence of team spirit...

Jess's legs felt like jelly as she turned into the stables. She knew what she had to do. The ponies stood ready for loading into the horseboxes, and the riders all looked smart and poised. Someone had already groomed Skylark, and she stood among them, calm and serene. There was Jasper, standing in the middle of it all, glancing anxiously around.

"Jess!" he cried. "Where have you been? I hope you haven't been getting last minute nerves!"

"I'm not nervous," Jess said as she took a deep breath, "because I'm not going to ride for you today. You can win your trophies without me."

"This is no time for jokes, Jess." Jasper's voice was calm, dangerous even. The others all stared at Jess in amazement.

"It's not a joke." Jess looked at Camilla and Lucy and Samantha and Allison and suddenly felt very certain. "I can't ride for Rychester," she said boldly. "I don't belong here. Skylark doesn't belong here. You're involved with things I'm ashamed of."

Jasper laughed scornfully. "You don't believe all that rubbish in the papers, do you?"

"Yes," Jess said firmly. "Yes, I do believe it, so I'm not riding today. I'm not riding for Rychester ever."

"But we won't be able to win the team event

without you," Camilla interrupted incredulously. "We need five riders." Her voice became wheedling. "And Skylark – she looks fantastic."

"She is fantastic." Jess was quietly confident. "But she's not competing."

Camilla's voice changed instantly, and now she spat out her words furiously. "I always thought you were a wimp, Jess. And you never deserved a place on our team anyway."

Jess shrugged her shoulders and turned away. Camilla was a selfish, spoilt girl. Her words, designed to cut, meant nothing to Jess.

"I warn you, Jess," Jasper continued. "If you leave us now, you're out of Rychester for good."

Jess walked over to her pony and put a hand on her neck. "Let's go, Skylark," she murmured.

"Hang on a minute." Jasper's voice was cold and controlled as he took a step towards her. "You're welcome to go but we're keeping Skylark. Do you think I wasted my time and money on an expensive show pony just so you could whisk her away?"

Jess froze. What was Jasper talking about?

"Skylark belongs to Rychester, Jess, and here she will stay."

"But…" Jasper's cold aggression left Jess feeling very small and alone. "But she's mine," she managed. "I won her."

"Legally Skylark is Rychester's," Jasper said. "For the year she's stabled here anyway. It's in the competition rules, if you read the small print. Now, if you'll excuse me, we've got a show to win… Mel!" Jasper called loudly to the stable girl. "Let's get these horses into the box. You'll be riding Skylark today."

Jess stood rooted to the spot, looking helplessly on as Skylark was led up the ramp and driven away. If only she had kept her mouth shut, Skylark would still be hers.

There was only one place she could go. Grabbing her bike, she flew out of the Rychester yard, pedalling furiously until she arrived, twenty minutes later, at Sandy Lane Stables. The familiar yard was bustling with riders and horses.

Suddenly shy, Jess pedalled slowly up the drive.

A puzzled Rosie looked up from where she was plaiting Pepper's mane. "Jess, what are you doing here? I thought we'd be seeing you at Ash Hill. We're just getting ready to go. Where's Skylark?"

"Jess, where've you been hiding?" Charlie cried.

"Hello Jess." Tom smiled at her. "Been jumping any more death traps recently?"

"Wrong stables, Jess!" called Nick, cheerfully.

It was all too much. Jess could hold the tears back no longer…

"Oh, Jess." Nick's face showed only concern as he tried to console her. "Come and get a drink at the cottage and tell me what's going on."

In a rush, Jess poured out everything that had happened – the news story, her decision not to ride at Ash Hill, Jasper's reaction, and finally the shocking news that Skylark wasn't really hers.

Nick sighed heavily and shook his head. "What a story," he said. "Jasper Carlisle sounds like a nasty piece of work. But I'm proud of you. For what it's worth, I think you've made the right decision."

"I thought I had," Jess squeaked miserably. "But what about Skylark? It looks as though I've lost her."

Nick glanced out of the window at the others getting ready for Ash Hill in the stable yard. He seemed to be weighing things up in his mind and it was a few minutes before he spoke again.

"Look, I don't know all the fine details about this competition," he said slowly. "But I've an idea of what we can say to Jasper. Right now, I need to take my riders to Ash Hill. Make sure you're here at 6 o'clock this evening and we'll drive to Rychester."

Jess's heart leapt and then sank. "Can't I come with you?" she pleaded.

"Sorry, Jess." Nick shook his head. "It's probably best if you stay away from the show today. It might be awkward if Jasper sees you there, and I don't want any scenes. Let's wait and tackle him tonight. Trust me on this one, OK?"

Jess was desperate to go to Ash Hill, frantic to see Skylark, but Nick had asked her to trust him and she would. As she followed Nick into the stable yard, Rosie raised her eyebrows enquiringly, but there was no time to talk.

"Come on, everybody," Nick was calling. "Let's get these horses loaded or we'll be late."

And for the second time that morning, Jess was left standing on her own in a stable yard, watching as a horsebox drove away to Ash Hill. She kicked her heels in the gravelled earth. It was going to be a long day. She'd told her parents she hadn't been picked to ride at Ash Hill, but they still thought she was going along to watch. She didn't feel like returning home and having to explain everything – not yet. She knew they would only worry.

Jess wandered back to the cottage. Nick's wife, Sarah, was there and she was sure to have plenty of Sandy Lane jobs to keep Jess busy...

Chapter 16

Showdown

At six that evening, Jess stood impatiently in the Sandy Lane yard. Finally, the horsebox rolled up the drive and there was a flurry of activity.

"Jess, I won!" Rosie cried. "Pepper and I won the Open Jumping."

"The Open Jumping? That's fantastic." Jess beamed. "How did Rychester do?"

"Not a rosette in sight." Rosie grinned. "They fell to pieces. The team event was won by a stables on the other side of Brookwood. You should have seen Jasper Carlisle. He was livid."

Jess couldn't believe what Rosie was telling her. Surely at least Camilla would have won something… Then Nick appeared. "Sorry, Jess, I was just making a phone call. All part of the plan," he said mysteriously as he opened the door of the Land Rover. "Right, are you ready to go?"

Jess nodded. What was Nick planning?

Nick kept up a steady stream of chatter on the way to Rychester, as if to put Jess at ease. "Rosie and Pepper jumped tremendously. The competition from Rychester wasn't very fierce after all. You should have seen the girl who was riding Skylark. She launched the pony at the first jump on far too tight a rein. Skylark wasn't having any of it and screeched to a halt. The girl went soaring over the jump and landed very unceremoniously on her bottom, while Skylark just stood there shaking her head and neighing loudly!"

Jess couldn't stop herself from laughing out loud.

They were still laughing as the Land Rover arrived at Rychester. The place looked deserted and Jess felt a sudden panic. What if Jasper had taken Skylark somewhere else? She raced over to her box and sighed with relief as Skylark gave a loud whinny. Jess saw Nick knocking on the office door. She gave Skylark a quick hug and ran over to join him.

"Come in." Jasper's voice came loud and clear. "Hello, can I help?" he asked.

Nick put out his hand and smiled politely. "I'm Nick Brooks, owner of Sandy Lane Stables."

"Sandy Lane. I've heard that name recently…" Jasper said. Then he caught sight of Jess, standing nervously behind Nick, and instantly scowled. "You've got a nerve showing your face around here."

"It's actually Skylark we've come about, Mr. Carlisle," Nick said, politely. "I understand Jess isn't able to keep Skylark here any more, so I've offered to keep the pony at Sandy Lane. We've come to collect her and settle any outstanding bills."

Jess gave a gasp. It was an excellent plan, but would Jasper allow it? Then she saw a malicious grin spread across his face.

"And who wouldn't want a pony as valuable as Skylark?" he ventured, his silvery voice still sounding pleasant. "But I'm afraid it's not quite as easy as that." Jasper picked up some official looking papers. "You see, Skylark legally belongs to Rychester."

He handed the papers to Nick, and smiled smugly at Jess. She felt suddenly faint. So this was it. Her dream really was over. Skylark was lost for ever...

Strangely, Nick didn't sound defeated. "I would have thought that with all the trouble your cosmetics company is in at the moment," he said calmly, "the last thing you need is more bad publicity."

"How dare you threaten me?" spat Jasper.

"Taking away a child's pony will hardly help improve your reputation," Nick went on.

"But the pony's mine," Jasper hissed.

"Carlisle the Pony Snatcher," a familiar voice rang out and everyone turned to see Penny Webster from the *Daily Advertiser* standing on the doorstep.

"What...?" Jasper began.

Penny smiled as she walked into the room.

"Thanks for the phone call, Mr. Brooks. You're right – the *Daily Advertiser* would be very interested in the story. Now let me see if I've got the facts straight." Penny flicked through her notebook. "Jasper Carlisle, owner of the disgraced cosmetics company, Vrai Vert, gives a pony away in a competition," she read. "But when the lucky winner decides – understandably after all that has happened – that she doesn't want to keep her pony on at Rychester, Mr. Carlisle announces that the pony isn't really hers at all." Penny looked up from her pad. "It's a mean trick to play on a child, don't you think? I can see the story on tomorrow's front pages."

"All right." Jasper held up his hand. "Have the pony. It disgraced me at Ash Hill today anyway. It's more trouble than it's worth. Just take it away and–"

"We'll say no more about it?" Nick said enquiringly.

"Exactly," Jasper spluttered. He sank down into his chair, suddenly looking very old. He clearly wasn't used to being defeated. "Now get out of here." Jasper pointed wearily at the door.

"If you could just sign here," Nick pointed to a space on the documents, "then we'll be quite happy to take the pony off your hands."

With a grimace, Jasper signed, and Jess, Nick and Penny left.

"Thanks for turning up here." Nick smiled at Penny. "I don't think Mr. Carlisle would have given in without you."

"That's OK," Penny said. "I'm glad things have worked out the way they have."

"Now how are we going to get you and Skylark back to Sandy Lane then?" Nick turned to Jess with a sparkle in his eye. "You won't both fit in the Land Rover."

Jess grinned back. She wanted to thank Nick, but she was speechless with happiness.

"Her tack's still here, I presume," Nick continued. "Do you think you could ride her back?"

"With pleasure!" said Jess, finding her voice at last. "Thanks, Nick…for everything."

Chapter 17

Home at Last

Jess leaned back on her brush the next day and surveyed the stable yard. Yes, the woodwork could do with a lick of paint but to Jess, Sandy Lane Stables looked perfect.

Jess had explained everything to her parents when she'd got home. They were relieved that Jess had escaped Rychester and delighted that Nick would cover the stabling costs in return for using Skylark in lessons.

Now, Skylark hung her head over the stable door, looking completely at home.

"Hi Jess." Rosie waved, cycling into the yard.

"Rosie…at last!" Jess grinned. "I want to hear all about Ash Hill. Nick said you rode brilliantly on Pepper, but whatever happened to Camilla Carlisle?"

"She really lost her rag!" Rosie chortled. "I heard her arguing with her dad just before her turn. She was all fired up…completely lost her composure. Her palomino refused three times at the wall, and almost bucked her off too."

"Good for Apollo." Jess laughed. "I wonder if Jasper will throw Camilla out for not winning!"

"Have you seen the *Daily Advertiser* headline article this morning?" Rosie asked.

"No, what is it now?" Jess asked warily.

"I couldn't resist buying a copy," Rosie smiled. She held it out for Jess to see.

Carlisle's Comeuppance! by *Penny Webster,* Jess read. *Vrai Vert Cosmetics, who were last week exposed for lying about their animal testing procedures, are today facing more problems. Protesters have mounted a vigil outside the company's laboratory in Greater*

Rychester. The protest organiser, Barry Watkins, said they wanted everyone in the country to be aware of the company's conduct. A spokesman for the company said this will undoubtably have an effect on sales. Jasper Carlisle, owner of Vrai Vert Cosmetics, was still unavailable for comment yesterday.

Jess looked thoughtful. "No one's going to want to keep their pony at Rychester now," she said.

"Let's hope Jasper sells the stables to someone who really cares about animals," Rosie added. "Anyway, I'm glad we've got you back, Jess, and now we've got Skylark too! Do you mind sharing her?"

"Not at all," Jess said quickly. "I thought I'd lost her for ever at one point. But now I know she'll always be mine, whoever rides her."

"Well you'd better get her tacked up," said Rosie. "It's nearly time for the 11 o'clock hack."

Jess grabbed Skylark's tack and headed to her pony's stall. "Hello, Skylark," she said. "I hope you're ready for a good gallop."

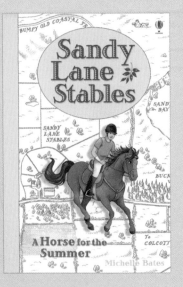

Sandy Lane Stables

A Horse for the Summer

Michelle Bates

Sandy Lane Stables

Ride by Moonlight

Michelle Bates

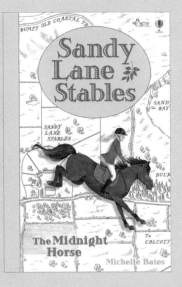

Sandy Lane Stables

The Midnight Horse

Michelle Bates